To Rosie

First published in Great Britain as **Trixie Tempest and the Amazing Talking Dog**
by HarperCollins **Children's Books** in 2003
This edition published by HarperCollins **Children's Books** in 2007
HarperCollins **Children's Books** is a division of HarperCollins**Publishers** Ltd,
77-85 Fulham Palace Road, Hammersmith, London W6 8JB

www.harpercollinschildrensbooks.co.uk

1

Text and illustrations copyright © Ros Asquith 2003

The author asserts the moral right to be identified
as the author of this work.

ISBN-13: 978-0-00-724402-7
ISBN-10: 0-00-724402-9

Printed and bound in England by
Clays Ltd, St Ives plc

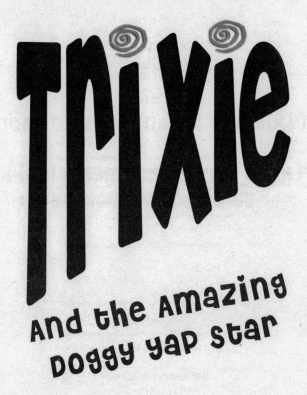

Trixie

And the Amazing Doggy Yap Star

ROS ASQUITH

HarperCollins *Children's Books*

Also by Trixie (with help from Ros Asquith):

TRiXie and DReam PONY OF DOOM

TRiXie's very extremely Brilliant guide to everything

Hi. My name's Trixie. You could spell it Tricksy, which would tell you more about me, but I reckon you get further by not giving the game away. Here's me:

You can see most of the things I've got, except the bits that are covered up by clothes, or inside my head but those are things I reckon I should keep to myself. Although I *am* willing to share *some* of the stuff in my head with you, as we get to know each other.

Most of what you can see, of course, isn't that unusual, and on the whole I'm glad about that. Such as, you know, one arm on each side, hands glued on to them by wrists with about sixty billion bracelets and bangles; two legs covered in sticky plasters, excellent kicking feet at the ends. I keep trying to get Dad to insure my feet for a zillion pounds as I am even better at free kicks than Bashful Becks himself. Then I could End My Career by falling off Tomato's tricycle at full speed and claim the money, even if I would have to pretend to walk with a limp for the rest of my life.

Tomato's my kid brother by the way: Very Extremely round, with a Very Extremely red face.

(I have no idea how he got the nickname Tomato.) Tomato is four and in nursery. There are no prisons for four-year-olds yet, except I think in Texas.

On top of my neck I keep my head, and on top of that – where other people have hair – I wear a scruffy yellowish straw-like rug. Tomato says it looks like the bottom of his gerbil's cage, but I like to think of it more as a nice field of hay. I usually put it in bunches but often I can't be bothered. I did it all up with beads once for World Save the Bead Day or something, but they fell out one by one, ping ping ping pingetty pingetty ping ping ping at school, during assembly. I've also got: sixty-two freckles approx, but more in summer. My eyes are weird. They go blue or grey or even greenish, according to the weather, sometimes one does and the other doesn't. Grandpa Tempest says it's witchy blood that has run straight through the family for seventeen generations, at least since the Horrific Period, or maybe the Thoracic Period, or even longer.

I've also got one baby tooth still in front that

looks Very Extremely odd between all my big teeth, like a polar bear cub standing among a lot of icebergs. My legs are thin and bendy like liquorice sticks and also a bit knobbly like twiglets. Grandma Clump is always trying to feed me up and complains that I don't eat enough

meat. But I tell her I don't want MORE meat, I don't want ANY meat! I tell her I was a horse in a previous life and do NOT want to be a cannibal. DiddlyOddlyDocuses, or whatever those long-necked dinosaurs are called, were about as big as tower blocks and they only ate plants. Gorillas only eat fruit and veg and look how big they are. Anyway, as well as gorilla food, I'm always scoffing pasta and potatoes and sweets and beans and stuff, so I should be bigger than a gorilla.

Here is my family tree, though it's one of my life's Big Disappointments to find out you can have one, but that you can't climb it.

Anyway, I realise now I'm lucky to be able to draw this family tree at all, 'cos I know some kids who don't even know who their own dad is. As you'll see when you turn over the page, my dad's side is a bit more lively than my mum's. My dad is a builder. He either has too many jobs so he is out all the time, or not enough so he is at home moaning. He has nice curly hair. He is also very tall, so maybe I'll be tall with nice curly hair one day, instead of being a midget under a haystack.

Mum is a teacher! YES! I have to admit it, even though it hurts. But she is a NICE teacher, except that it means she never has enough time to see me and come into my school and do all the things other mums and dads do, like talk to the teacher and stuff, because she is always having to

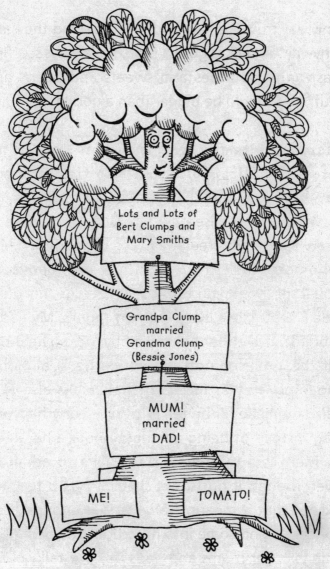

Lots and Lots of
Bert Clumps and
Mary Smiths

Grandpa Clump
married
Grandma Clump
(Bessie Jones)

MUM!
married
DAD!

ME!

TOMATO!

My Family Tree on MUM's side

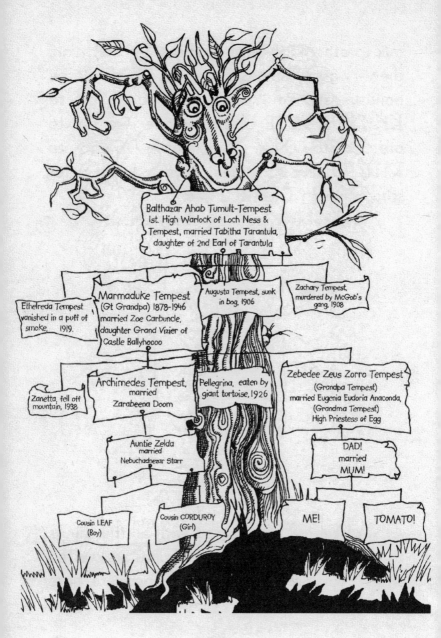

Balthazar Ahab Tumult-Tempest
1st. High Warlock of Loch Ness &
Tempest, married Tabitha Tarantula,
daughter of 2nd Earl of Tarantula

Ethelreda Tempest vanished in a puff of smoke, 1919.

Marmaduke Tempest (Gt Grandpa) 1878-1946 married Zoe Carbuncle, daughter Grand Vizier of Castle Ballyhoooo

Augusta Tempest, sunk in bog, 1906

Zachary Tempest, murdered by McGob's gang, 1908

Zanetta, fell off mountain, 1938

Archimedes Tempest, married Zarabeena Doom

Pellegrina, eaten by giant tortoise, 1926

Zebedee Zeus Zorro Tempest (Grandpa Tempest) married Eugenia Eudoria Anaconda, (Grandma Tempest) High Priestess of Egg

Auntie Zelda married Nebuchadnezar Starr

DAD! married MUM!

Cousin LEAF (Boy)

Cousin CORDUROY (Girl)

ME!

TOMATO!

talk to other kids' parents about THEM! Still, the very good thing is that she is around all the holidays and so I don't have to go off to KIDZFUNKLUB that everyone else has to pretend to enjoy. I do have to go to KIDZFUNKLUB three days a week after school though. GRRR. Unfair.

Now here is a drawing of my brain:

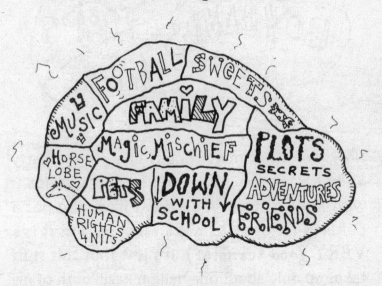

As you see, it is not stuffed with all the things that adults think tweenagers' brains are stuffed with. If you are wondering what those are, here is another picture of a brain, stolen at massive risk to Life and Limb from the Deepest, Darkest Depths of an Adult Imagination while it was asleep.

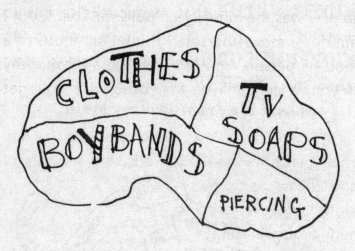

Now, don't get me wrong. I like a disco party as much as the next girl. I *have* got jeans with flowers down the sides. I have also got a butterfly tattoo (OK, not a real one, but it is a VERY good transfer). It's just that this stuff takes up only about one million kazillionth of my brain. The rest of it is full of boiling, frothing, glittering, fireworky stuff that isn't about TV or pop stars and all, whatever.

I go to St Aubergine's Primary School.

Unfortunately I am the smallest as well as the thinnest in my class, so in class photos I look like a pea in a potato field. In *Cinderella*, all I got to play was the mouse who pulls the coach. But I am not a mousy person. I think I am more of a mouthy person. You've got to be a bit mouthy if you're as small as me, otherwise you get stepped on.

My best friends are in the same class as me. They are **Chloe Caution** who is kind and careful and always has about eight bags of sweets hung around her waist under her jumper. She is so quiet and such a "wouldn't-say-boo-to-a-goose" sort of person that none of the teachers ever guess she is basically the Main Munch for the whole school; the sweet dealer everybody is Just Like That with.

This bulge is secret SWEETY supply

Chloe Caution
Quiet but nice

Dinah Dare-deVille
Naughty but nice

My other best-friend is **Dinah Dare-deVille** who is the eggzact opposite, always noisy. She'll be a famous actress, it's a certainty. She can copy other people's voices so well that half the time teachers don't know it's her that's done a Dirty Deed. She makes people think they're shouting Terrible Things out loud they didn't even know they knew in a whisper. But the other half of the time, the teachers know Dinah Dare-deVille's game all too well. That's why she is in detention more than any other girl in school. Well, you know, not detention like in Big School, but made to stay in at playtime and all, whatever.

But my biggest friend in the whole world is my dog, Harpo. Very Extremely big in fact. She is as fat as a hot-air balloon just now (and if you get close to one end of her, you'd realise I didn't just fall over this comparison without meaning it (corwhodidthat???!!!). Harpo is currently in love with Next-Door's big, handsome red setter who I suppose is quite a catch, or maybe a dogtch. He has a noble, pointy face like a dog in an old painting. He doesn't take much interest in Harpo though. She just looks like a dog in an old basket. It's like *The Lady and the Tramp* backwards. He's called (wait for it) Lorenzo! But though my dog may not win first prize in a Ms Pooch competition, she is one truly amazing dog, as you will find out very soon.

Anyway, that's enough about me and stuff for now. Except, oh ho, how could I forget? There are two humungously big loves in my life: HORSES – I am saving up to buy my own. And MUSIC! I play the trumpet! More about that later... because now, here is an incredibly TRUE story to tell you about Harpo. Sit back and you will be truly amazed. Money back if not. Well, maybe not that. You can write me a rude letter instead and I'll send you my autograph which will be worth at least one penny in the future, when I am a World Famous Author, Olympic Horse Riding Champion, captain of Euro FC PLC and First Child President of the World.

Chapter 1

My dog Harpo can talk. Believe it or not, it's true.

This is HARPO.

Some smart-looking dog isn't she? Yes, I know Harpo's a strange name for a dog, but she's a strange dog. She's never made a single sound since the day we found her – not a growl, or a whimper or a yap or a snore or the tiniest, whisperiest hint of a bark. So my parents named her after some character they liked who played the harp but never talked, in an old film made about a million years ago, when the dinosaurs were just settling in to Rule the World.

Mum found Harpo abandoned in a park. She was more a scrap of matted fur than a dog. She 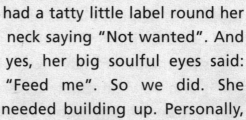 had a tatty little label round her neck saying "Not wanted". And yes, her big soulful eyes said: "Feed me". So we did. She needed building up. Personally, I'm a vegetarian because I have a mission to Save the World. But you can't make a dog a vegetarian; it isn't natural. So we fed her a diet of Fidoburgers and she came on a treat. You've probably seen those ads where a very cool-looking Labrador driving a sports car pulls up at a Fidoburger drive-in, collects his kingsize with extra bones on the side, and finds that three gorgeous girlie Labradors in crop tops and shades have hopped in the car to share it with him. "Fidoburgers put your dog a nose ahead!"

Well, I'm not one to buy everything I see advertised on the telly, but I have to say that though Harpo doesn't have a sports car and certainly doesn't have three hunky dogs in tow (I think I'd be jealous), she has turned pretty fast from a brillo pad into a brillo pillow, and this same Harpo, dog-of-my-dreams, can talk.

It started this very morning before breakfast. Harpo was helping out, as usual. She is a sleepy kind of pooch most of the time, and I don't deny she is on the plump side – well, fat, really – but she is also Very Extremely clever for a dog, and very extraordinarily good at stuff dogs do in books but hardly ever do in real life, like fetching slippers and the morning paper.

Harpo *always* fetches my Dad's slippers. He usually has to dry them out on the radiator afterwards, but he still likes the fact that she's done it. She fetches his paper too, and mostly she manages to avoid biting a hole in the bit Dad wants to read, which I think is another sign of her brilliance and advanced reading age. She can SIT as well, and sometimes so long after you told her to it's amazing how well she remembers.

This morning she was fetching the slippers and she came in with only one.

"Where's Dad's other slipper?" I asked her, expecting her to go back and look for it.

And she looked up really high, pointing her nose right up as if peering into a Far Distant Universe where the planets were made only of Fidoburgers and she went: "WOOF."

Now, you could say, that's just the noise dogs make, but she'd never made it before, so for her it was a miracle. And there was something about the way she kept staring upwards as she made it. It couldn't possibly be, I thought to myself, that she's trying to say "roof" could it?

"You mean it's on the roof?" I asked her, as one does. And Harpo nodded!

I shouted upstairs to Dad. "Where's your other slipper Dad?"

Harpo looked round at me with a Very Extremely chilled-out look, as if to say "I've TOLD you already, you numbbum."

It seemed like a long time before Dad's voice came back. "I lost it on the roof. It fell into a gutter where I couldn't reach it while I was trying to recover the football you so thoughtfully kicked up there."

YESSS, I knew it! I had a talking dog! A hound with a sound! A muttering Mutt! A conversing canine!

First thing I did next was to visit Harpo in her basket, where she had already sloped off for her early morning nap. Harpo has a lot of naps. In fact they all seem to join together to make one long nap. (Why are they called catnaps?) Her eyes were fast shut, but her tail was revolving like a windmill. Obviously, she was dreaming about Next-Door's cat. Or maybe Lorenzo, their big handsome red setter.

"Wake up Harpo, just for a minute, this is really important."

She opened one eye. I swore I could see Lorenzo in her eyeball. Maybe it's my seventeen generations of witchy blood on my dad's side that has made me a Mind Reader.

"Harpo. Listen carefully. Where did you say Dad's other slipper was?"

"Woof," she went.

I decided to get really sneaky.

"What's that brown stuff around the outside of the tree trunks you wee against?"

"Bark," said she, clear as clear.

Keep an eye out for that dog of mine, that's all I can say. You'll see her on TV before long.

She'll be the world's first Yap Artist. She'll be on Top of the Pups. She'll make Snoop Doggy Dogg start to think what a dog's life is really all about. Maybe she'll get her own late-night Yap Show. Make Michael Parkinson come onto the stage on all fours.

Then the fireworks started going off in my brain. **A PLAN** was taking shape – a plan to make ALL my dreams come true. Everyone from miles around would flock to see **HUMUNGOUS HARPO, THE AMAZING TALKING DOG!** And I'd get them to PAY to hear her!

It won't be for me you know, well not entirely. Let me tell you how I feel about money. Whenever I get some, a quarter goes straight into my noble, selfless Caring for Others fund – it could be, you know, Save the Whale campaigns, or jewellery for friends or Christmas presents. Some goes for comics and sweeties, of course. Half goes straight into my MERLIN fund, which is a BIG SECRET I'll tell you about as long as you promise not to tell anybody else. The MERLIN fund is not about magic. Merlin is my best pet of all but don't tell Harpo. He is palomino (that is

gold with a cream mane and tail for those of you ignorant un-horsey types) and he can jump a two-metre fence and gallop like the wind. He's got a cowboy saddle and bridle and he only lets ME ride him because he is like a Very Extremely wild bucking bronco with anyone else.

Well, I haven't actually got him as such yet. But I'm saving up loads of money (£47.84p so far) to get him. I'll tell you when I do. Well, I won't need to. You'll hear me, as I ride him, laughing into the wind, wherever you are in the world.

So carrying my brain full of fireworks down to breakfast with me on the morning I discovered that Harpo can talk, I decided to be sneaky and clever about my amazing news.

"Hey hey hey MUM!" I shouted, "Harpo can talk!"

"That's nice, dear" she replied, but she wasn't listening. She was stirring her coffee with a pen that was steadily turning it blue, and sometimes stopping in mid-stir to stare sadly at her left hand and wipe her eye with the right.

Full of thoughts of the Talking Harpo as I was, I still couldn't help wondering what was up, so I asked her.

"It's my Diamond Togetherness Ring. Gone," she whispered tragically.

"Not your Diamond Togetherness Ring!"

"My Diamond Togetherness Ring. Not together."

Dad gave Mum this Precious Thing when they had been together for a year and their love was young. He forgot to ever give her a wedding ring, so this one is specially important.

"I think Dad sucked it up in the floor sander when he was doing the bathroom," Mum said in despair, sipping her blue coffee.

Maybe this wasn't the best time to introduce the subject of a talking dog. This was painful to me, because I've never wanted to tell somebody about something as much, ever. But you have to live and let live, and you have to keep your mouth shut when the time isn't right to open it, too. At this moment maybe it was better to change the subject to something Mum might possibly be interested in, her children starving for instance and getting their pictures on telly as a Human Tragedy on Red Nose Day. The packet of Krispy Popsickles (Hear them Popsicrackle! Hear them Popsipop! Once you start Popsickling, you'll never stop!), on which I depend to keep body and soul together, was empty.

Tomato's bowl, on the other hand, was Very Extremely full.

"Are there any more Krispy Popsickles?" I asked, sadly waving the packet about.

"Hmmm. I'll ask your teacher," Mum said without listening.

"But Tomato's got a whole bowlful!"

"Hear Popshicrackle! Hear Popshipop! Once shtart Popshickling, never shtop!" Tomato chanted smugly. Then he put both hands in the bowl, raised them to his round red face, and suddenly they were all gone. I was surprised even the bowl was left.

"He's ate them all!"

"Eaten them all, darling. Never mind, there's some nice muesli," said Mum. She examined the sell-by date, which was some time before Jesus. "Muesli can't go off," she muttered, pouring out some stuff that looked like floor sweepings.

"There MUST be some more Krispy Popsickles somewhere! Didn't we buy six packets for the price of four only last week?"

But Mum was busy marking homework.

"Dad, have you seen the Krispy Popsickles?"

Dad staggered into the kitchen carrying a plank. Despite the sixteen generations of witchy blood coursing through his veins, Dad has trouble handling two things at once; like a question and a plank. So when I asked him about the Krispy Popsickles he turned the plank sideways to put it down, which swept a lot of even older cereal packets with sell-by dates Before Dinosaurs off the dresser on to the floor, and quite a lot of cups and plates and stuff came clattering down as well. Most of them broke in the places where Dad had Superglued them last time, so not too

Whoopsy

much harm was done. Dad kicked them under the dresser "for later", scooped up a few greenish flakes of muesli and bits of crockery from the floor and shook them into my bowl. "Spit 'em out if you get any sharp bits," he muttered, parking his plank and sitting down with the paper.

"Harpo can talk, Dad," I told him.

"See the Germans are at it again," he said to nobody in particular, frowning at the headline.

Mum looked at the date. 1939. "I keep telling you to throw your dad's old newspapers out," she told him.

"Thank God for that," Dad said with relief. "Building an air-raid shelter would've taken at least till Monday week, always supposing you could still get the stuff."

Mum absent-mindedly wiped her eyes with the last bit of toast. I practised my witchy hypnoty technique willing her to replace the toast on the plate: "YOU DO NOT NEED OR WANT THAT TOAST. THAT TOAST DOES NOT NEED OR WANT YOU. IT WILL BE SAD AND LONELY IN YOUR TUMMY. IT WANTS TO BE EATEN BY YOUR LITTLE GIRL." I said that Very Extremely powerfully in my head, staring violently at the toast. But the toast, or my mum, didn't care, as her mouth opened and the toast popped in, as happily as if it were popping out of the toaster. That's it then, no breakfast.

At least Harpo cares. She came in and put her vast head in my lap. Harpo cares. And so do her fleas which leapt about all over me in a happy welcoming dance of recognition. I gave Harpo a big hug and sneezed about five thousand times.

"We must do something about your sneezing dear," said Mum. "Perhaps we should get rid of Harpo."

"NEVER!" I cried, scooping up my beloved dog and crashing backwards off my stool to the mouldy-cereal-strewn floor. I keep forgetting Harpo weighs a ton.

"You ought to go to school," Mum said, finishing her blue coffee and ignoring the *You've*

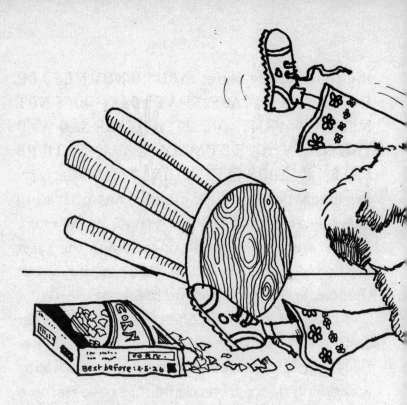

Been Framed-type situation thrashing around on the floor before her.

"So ought you," I told her, struggling to get an already snoozing Harpo off me and stand up.

"I'm on a course today," Mum said, staring moodily at her ringless finger again.

"Is anyone thinking of taking me to school?" I asked mournfully at this point.

"Sigh," went my mum.

"Sigh," went my dad.

"Time you started going in by yourself," they said.

"Whaaat?" I said. "I have to take my trumpet in today. We've got rehearsals for the *Save the World with a Song* concert all week, and I've got a solo in the bit where Rita Renewable, Goddess of the Future comes on."

The trumpet is one of the very few things I'm very good at, and though my music teacher says I ought to practise more (they all say that), I'm in our school band and it's one of the things I wouldn't miss even if an asteroid was due to hit the Earth five minutes into the first tune.

"Sorry," said Mum, only half listening. "I got to school without help on my own much younger than you and anyway, if you're a real musician, you ought to get used to turning up at shows properly equipped and on time by yourself."

So somehow I managed it. I got to school on time and without losing my precious trumpet that Mum and Dad bought me for about a squillion pounds, or leaving it on the bus or anything. It was like a little victory in a Cruel World, and for about a minute and a half it made me feel v good indeed. And if my own family didn't want to hear my news about the Amazing Talking Dog, I knew who would.

Chapter 2

Dinah and Chloe are the kind of people you could trust with Your Life; who wouldn't go round with a satellite TV link so they could tell the world what a prunella you were as soon as you told them a secret. We scarpered straight up to my room after school and locked the door, leaving Tomato screaming his nut off outside. I bribed him with a whole bag of Cyanide Schnozzlebursts, so we could have five minutes' peace with Harpo.

Trixie's Den

NO ENTRY

Keep OUT!

PRIVATE

Boo!

Harpo, as usual, wanted five hours' peace on her own and was snoozing in Dogland, tail gently flicking.

"Isn't she FAT?" said Dinah.

"You mean BIG," said Chloe crossly. Chloe is not exactly a knitting needle herself.

"No, but she has got bigger," said Dinah.

Harpo does look like an ad for dog mountain. Never mind. At least I know how to wake her up. "Lorenzo," I whispered meanly in her ear, and her eyes popped open in joyful hope, only to cloud in disappointment. I think Harpo used to love me, before Mrs Next-Door got that mutt.

"OK Harpo," I said, "what's that thing on the top of the house called?"

"WOOF," she went, right on cue.

"YES!"

"Would you say this is rough or smooth?" I said, putting her paw on my Brillo pad of a wig.

"RUFF!" she went.

"What's your favourite music?"

"BARK!"

"See? She's saying Bach," I said. "She listens when my mum's got Radio 3 on. She's in seventh heaven then."

But for the first time I felt a twinge of doubt.

"Cool," said Dinah.

But I knew what Chloe was thinking.

"Humph," said Chloe.

"What do you mean, 'Humph'?" I asked.

"Well, what dog doesn't go 'woof' and 'bark'?" asked Chloe, looking at me like a scientist examining a sheep dropping.

BUT THEN—

"Should I have said Mozart?" asked a voice.

"WHAAAAT?" we all went. Our jaws were on the floor. Really.

Because it wasn't my voice, or Chloe's or Dinah's. It was a warm, round, fat DOGGY voice.

It was Harpo.

"Or Beethoven? Or Robbie Williams?" Harpo continued. "Sorry, but I prefer the classics," she said.

She was looking at us with what I swear was a smile. Then a yawn. Then she nodded off completely. It was comforting, in some ways, to know she was still the same old Dozy Doggy underneath.

"This is, without doubt, a miracle," said Dinah. "This has never happened before. This is Canine History in the making. This is History in the Making, period."

"Most unusual, certainly," said Chloe, looking completely stunned and rather pale.

Me, I couldn't believe my ears. Look, I wasn't born yesterday. I wanted to kid my mates, and even myself, that Harpo could talk. But now it was real! She really could!

"We've got to handle this very, very carefully," said Chloe, very, very cautiously. "Don't tell anyone! We've got to make a plan! This will change our lives, and we want to make sure we're in control every step of the way! We have to swear a vow of secrecy, till we work out what to do."

"Why?" I asked. I wanted to tell the whole world about my amazing pet.

"Because everyone will want Harpo when they know she can speak, you airhead," said

Chloe crossly. "She'll be stolen by dognappers as soon as you can say 'woof'."

A cold chill chilled me. So we made a solemn vow:

"We swear by Dalmatian,
We swear by Alsatian,
We swear by collie and corgi and peke.
We swear on the Hound of the Baskervilles,
This Secret we will never speak!"

OK, it isn't Shakespeare, but if you can do better than that on the spur of the moment, send me your vow on a postcard and I'll send you a half-eaten pack of Fidoburgers with Harpo the Amazing Doggy Yap Star's actual real slobber on it!

I was in dreamland already, surrounded by Merlin, about fifty other horses, two football teams, a golden trumpet and my own private jewellery and sweetie empire. All the things that would be possible if the world knew about Harpo.

But a terrible doubt gnawed at me, just like Harpo gnawing the side-dish of a Fidoburger, only more anxious.

Could we really do this to her? It's exploitation

of innocent animals, isn't it? It's not fair. They're entitled to a life too, free from interviews and photographers and appearances on *Jonathan Ross*. A life of innocence and peace.

"Want more schnozzles!" yelled Tomato, battering at the door. Tomato is like a tank. He can break a door down if deprived of food for more than a few seconds. He should audition for *Superman – the Early Years*. Only a little bit of training and he'd be one of those disgusting bulgy blokes doing important things like lifting twenty-ton trucks and chucking them through hoops.

"Come on, Tom-Tom, I got a nice dog biccy here," I said, letting my poor little round red weeping brother in.

But at the words "dog biccy" Harpo was alert like a swooping eagle and snaffled it just as Tomato put out his little sticky paw.

"Notty Harpo, baddog," said Tomato, hurling himself at her and trying to prise open her jaws. "Harpo sillydog. Not talkin'."

"Does she talk to you too, Tomato?" said Dinah, amazed.

"Me an' Harpo talk about EVERYTHING," said Tomato smugly, managing to suck a crumb of dog biscuit off Harpo's whiskers. She had fallen asleep again straight away. It's amazing how she does that.

"Tom-Tom, why didn't you tell me Harpo could talk?" I asked.

"Never lissen me," said Tomato, putting on his best pathetic face. Which was true, I guess.

"Don't tell Mum and Dad, will you?" I wheedled. "Let this be our big secret Tom-Tom?"

(I reluctantly gave him my spare bucket of Cyanide schnozzles as I said this.)

"Fish fingers!" shouted Mum.

"Now remember, say nothing to Mum!" I warned Tomato as we hurtled downstairs.

"Mum! Harpo talkin'!" shouted Tomato, as Dinah, Chloe and me flattened him. It takes three of us, believe me.

"Mum, Dad. Harpo talkin' me. She says Tixie **VERY** bad dog." Tomato repeats cheerfully at tea.

"That's nice, dear," said Mum, gazing more wistfully than ever at her ringless finger.

"Never lissen me," said Tomato, chomping his way through eight fish fingers.

Just as well, I thought, trying to squeeze the last drop of ketchup.

Why use ONE fork when two are quicker?

Ulp. That very night I dreamt I was on the *Titanic*, which was, of course, sinking. Then just as I was getting into a lifeboat, this monster the size of a forest jumped on me. And when I woke up, there was a Very Extremely real monster on top of me! A big hairy mountainous dribbling slavering hairy hot molten toothy **MONSTER!**

"A MONSTER!" I was dying! "Help! Mum! Dad! It's huge and hairy!" I wasn't quite dead yet! "Only a few seconds and I'm dead! HELP! These are the last words I'll ever speak!"

Only one second—

"A -TISHOOO!!!!!"

Of course, those weren't the last words I ever spoke. Well, if they had been, I couldn't have written this, could I? Any dumbbell can see that.

Where was I? I know, I wanted to tell you about being eaten by a monster. Rather than the last words I spoke, they were actually the FIRST words I spoke, that very next morning, after Harpo had gone on about Robbie Williams and such.

It was at about two a.m. to be exact, that time of morning when nothing's going on anywhere except that the house is creaking and groaning and sloshing about, and your head is full of thoughts of all the stuff wandering about in all the nooks and crannies. Creepy-crawlies and meeces, rats and spiders and bedbugs blown up the size they show on the Discovery Channel so they look like mechanical diggers with legs.

Usually, in order not to be scared out of my wits by all this stuff, I sensibly take avoiding action and sleep as deep and fast and inky-black as I possibly can. But then the MONSTER leapt upon me, squeezing the very breath out of my tiny frame.

In case you hadn't guessed, it wasn't a monster. It was Harpo, who was sleeping on my head.

"Why did you do that, Harpo?" I asked, pushing her, ever so gently, to the end of the bed. It was like pushing an elephant; she is fatter than ever.

But, you know, she just went "grrrfwll", like a completely ordinary dog.

For the second time, I began to wonder if I'd imagined the whole thing. But Dinah and Chloe had been **THERE.** They'd heard it all. I finally fell asleep again, dreaming that the *Titanic* had collided with a ginormous dog-shaped iceberg made of frozen dog-wee, and that my lifeboat was drifting down and down into the unspeakably murky depths...

"Take care of Harpo, Dad," I said, in a fog of sleeplessness, the next morning. I was strangely worried that somehow the secret would leak out of my head, or out of Chloe and Dinah's heads, and dribble along the floor, out of the door and into the ears of local burglars who would come and nab my Amazing Talking Pet.

"Mmmm," said Dad, who by a weird and witchy coincidence was reading about the Titanic in a 1926 copy of *The Times*.

"Why are you reading that?" asked Mum.

"No holes," muttered Dad. "Couldn't we get a decent dog without teeth?" he said, turning to the shredded bits of today's paper he'd rather have been reading.

"Don't say that!" I squeaked, putting my hands over Harpo's ears. "She needs her teeth to t—"

I nearly said "talk". Am I going mad?

"Tear holes in my paper?" asked Dad.

"Be NICE to Harpo! She isn't very well."

"She's too fat. She needs more exercise," muttered Dad.

"And fewer Fidoburgers," said Mum.

"You're all horrible," I cried, kissing Harpo, who looked quite depressed. "They love you really," I whispered to her. But did they? If they knew she could understand every word they said, what would they think?

"Have a good day dear," said Mum. "It's so nice you're getting so independent now."

I went to school by bus again, almost asleep. If it hadn't been for the strange toothless old man sitting next to me, who smelt of drink even though it was eight-thirty in the morning, and who I was sure was looking at me in a weird and creepy way, I would probably have dozed off there and then and ended up halfway round the world. I wanted to move to another part of the bus but there wasn't any room.

I was so glad when I reached the school stop and got off. I could see his whiskery face looking blearily through the window at me as the bus rumbled off down the road.

Then I got a horrible empty feeling deep down in the bottom of my stomach. I had my bag. I had my packed lunch. I had my arms and legs and spiky wig, but I didn't have my sleepy feeling any more. Because I didn't have my precious trumpet any more either.

I'D LEFT IT ON THE BUS.

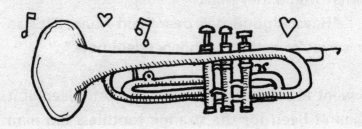

Chapter 3

How can life be so unfair? Just when you find the most wonderful thing that ever happened to you in your life, up pops the worst thing that ever happened at almost exactly the same time. It's unbelievable.

At lunch time Dinah and Chloe soon spotted something was up.

"What's happened?" Dinah asked. "Has Harpo told you she can't stand the sight of you? That's the trouble when your dog starts talking."

"She hasn't talked since," I said, gloomily.

"She will," said Dinah encouragingly. "It's no reason to be so upset."

"It's not the reason," I said after a long while.

"What is it then?" she asked.

"It's my trumpet."

"Your TRUMPET?! The one your mum and dad spent a squillion pounds on?"

"Yes. That one. I lost it on the bus coming to school."

"The BUS? You left it on the BUS?"

This was beginning to sound like little Sir Echo.

"Yes. The bus. What am I going to do? The *Save the World with a Song* show is in two weeks' time and I haven't got a trumpet. What am I supposed to do, hold a sink plunger to my mouth and imitate one? And it's not just that. I could say I was sick on the concert day, even though I've been looking forward to it for weeks and it's a chance to do something that shows I care. But it's Mum and Dad. Mum's just lost her Diamond Togetherness Ring, the last thing they're going to do now is pay for another trumpet."

Dinah had a look on her face I'd seen before.

"We can get you that money," she said, quietly.

"How?" I asked.

"Are you daft or what?" Dinah said. "What did you tell me only yesterday was the most amazing piece of good news you'd ever had?"

You know those films where the heroine is clinging to the remains of the little rope bridge over the raging torrent below, and the strands of the rope are snapping one by one? And then James Bond, or Hagrid-on-a-motorbike, or Indiana Jones in a helicopter that he only just learned to fly that second, stretches out an effortless mitt and grabs her as the last string breaks with a twang and a big ba-DOOM from the cunningly hidden orchestra? That's the scene I suddenly saw in just that moment.

Because Dinah was talking about... Harpo the HUMUNGOUS HOLLERING HOUND!

And when you think about it like that, the cruel world can start to look quite a bit different. A TALKING DOG? What would people pay to hear a TALKING DOG? Obviously a big lot of money. Maybe enough big lots of money for me to get another trumpet in time for the *Save the World with a Song* concert. Maybe enough even for me to Save Mum and Dad's Happiness and get another Diamond Togetherness Ring. Maybe EVEN enough for me to Save the Rainforest, Save the Poor Peoples of The World, Save the Ozone Layer – well, just Save Everything Needing Saving really, and be the biggest Superhero that ever lived.

Hang on, I think I'm running a bit ahead of myself here.

First off, we had to see if Harpo really was up to the challenge of rescuing me from financial ruin. Dinah and Chloe agreed to come round immediately after school to help organise it, and in Harpo's case such a thing needs a lot of organising. As usual, Harpo was fast asleep and refused to say a word to me at first. Tomato was banned from the room. This meant setting him up with a trough of sweets and an unsuitable video (*Squid Attack Two*, in which a giant squid the length of our street viciously drags innocent seafarers to their Doom until befriended by a small boy who teaches it to do tricks like spinning plates on the ends of its tentacles, well, something like that anyway).

But the minute Dinah appeared, Harpo just came ALIVE. They obviously have a wonderful understanding, it almost makes me envious. How could this happen when she's known dear Harpo for a fraction of the time that I have?

"How many dogs does it take to change a light bulb?" asked Dinah.

"We've got our whole lives ahead of us, there's a fat bone to chew, a newspaper to read and then eat, a bag of Fidoburgers waiting to be snaffled and a bed waiting to be slept on – and all you care about is a light bulb?" said Harpo.

We were amazed.

Harpo, THE INCREDIBLE QUIPPING CANINE!!

Then she sang the first lines of the entire TOP TEN!

Harpo, THE INCREDIBLE MUSICAL MUTT.

Then she started to recite *The Walrus and the Carpenter*, (except she changed it into *The Wolfhound and the Corgi*) which is a very funny, but Very Extremely long poem that nice Mrs Muse, the visiting Literacy teacher, has been trying to make us learn all term.

Harpo, THE INCREDIBLE POETIC POOCH.

And I swear Harpo laughed her head off. Though she might have been yawning. Then she fell asleep and even Dinah couldn't wake her.

Harpo THE INCREDIBLE DOZING DOG.

Whooooopppeeeeee!
I am beginning to think
we could actually make
something out of Harpo's
extraordinary talent.

But how?

"She has to do a show," Dinah said. "She has to do a public performance and we have to sell tickets for it. That's how we'll raise the money for your trumpet."

I looked doubtfully at the Incredible Dozing Dog. "It's not really fair on her is it?" I said. "I mean, we're pushing her into it for our own selfish ends. And anyway, she's asleep most of the time."

"Don't call us selfish," Dinah said, looking at Chloe, and on the edge of a huff. "We're only trying to help."

"I know, I know, you're right," I said. It obviously was the only way out. "But how will we do it? And where? Maybe the Empire Ballroom, Brixton Academy, Buckingham Palace, the Stadium of Light, the Albert Hall, Hackney Empire?"

"We couldn't afford them," Chloe said regretfully. "And they wouldn't let us anyway. They'd say we'd stick chewing gum under the tables or tread crisps into the carpets or draw on the walls or leave the back door open or something."

"We'll use my house," said Dinah suddenly.

"WHAAAT?" said Chloe and me together.

"My house. There's loads of space. We won't have to pay a single penny to use it. We could get kazillions of audiences in. And next Saturday my Mum and Dad are going off all day to a wedding miles away and won't be back till late. They're leaving me with Dora."

Dora is Dinah's Big Sister. Unfortunately she is like a teacher in the body of a sixteen-year-old, which might be a problem.

"We won't tell her until Saturday morning. After my parents have left. Then it'll be too late," Dinah said, grinning. "She might be like a teacher, but she's like a v. weedy one. She won't have the bottle to tell all those people to go home when they start showing up at the door."

"We need posters," Chloe said, pondering. "So people know it's on."

"But we can't say it's at my place," Dinah said, sadly. "My Mum and Dad or Dora might see them, then it'd be all over."

"I know," I said, my brain clanking and whirring into action, "we can say, 'Come to the post office and a guide will bring you to the show'."

"Who're we going to use as a guide?"

"One of us, of course. Not me, as I will be busy holding Harpo's paw."

"Supposing it's *pawing* with rain?"

"Don't be so wet!"

"Har Har!"

"Anyway, it's a stupid idea. It'll sound really suspicious. People won't come, they'll think we're kidnappers and stuff," Chloe said, right as usual. "We'll just have to put the posters up on Saturday morning where your parents won't see them."

"YES!"

"YES!"

So then we decided eggzactickly what to do. We would design posters in every spare minute.

Then we would choose the best design, print it up on Dinah's mum's computer and plaster them all over every tree in the neighbourhood. There wasn't much time before Harpo's Big Show. So we had to get on with them in school time, which was pretty tricky.

Unfortunately my first two poster designs were confiscated by our horrendous supply teacher, Warty-Beak.

As he approached, I tried desperately to cover up my poster and get on with evil Maths, such as, "If Tania has two apples and Harpinder has four, how many apples has Sagrid?" HOW are you supposed to know that?

Unfortunately, we were supposed to be doing a picture of the life cycle of a butterfly. Whoopsy. Science. Not Maths.

Warty-Beak in very good mood

So, I convinced Warty-Beak that I was slaving over a hot butterfly cycle by working out the time it took for a larva to hatch its egg or whatever it is they do and he scuttled away, shading his robot-red eyes against the Invincible Power of my Pink Belt in deadly Fu-Mathsu. Hah! A cunning yet oh-so-simple trick that you too can learn if you read every word of this book and are able to recite it all backwards while standing on your head. (Not REALLY!)

Warty-Beak then scuttled to the other side of the classroom to examine the dogapult (So? I like dogs more than cats) that Dennis and Sumil have built out of broken pencils and pants' elastic. They were using it to fire bits of Lego into the infants' playground, but the infants didn't mind – they just picked it all up to build a twenty-eight-legged dinosaur with a blue mobile phone mast sticking out of its head.

dogapult

Lego dinosaur

Then I heard the crackling old voice of Warty-Beak saying: "What is that? A Talking DOG?"

But the voice was SO crackly and sizzly and Warty, that I just KNEW it was Dinah, pretending to be him. Dinah is the world's best mimic, I kid-you-not. So I said, "Shut up, batface," but unfortunately it wasn't Dinah it was Warty-Beak himself and no other. Whoopsy. It is lucky he is quite deaf.

"Is that the life cycle of a caterpillar, Patricia?" he asked.

Ug. Patricia! I go red as Tomato when anyone calls me that.

Warty-Beak leant over and peered at my page.

"Harpo seems an unusual name for a caterpillar," he hissed, rasping his claws together and lashing his scaly tail.

"It's the butterfly's name, Warty-B— I mean, Mr..."

But Sumil and Dennis were sitting right behind Warty-Beak at the moment he bent over my page and they were making Very Extremely rude faces. Before my brain could clank and whirr enough to remind me that any face I made in return might look like it was aimed at Warty-Beak, I stuck my tongue out really far like an anteater and curled it. This always makes Sumil and Dennis go bananas because they can't curl their tongues. But one look at the livid snout of Warty-Beak made my tongue snap back as though on a elastic band. Too late. Warty-Beak has Very Extremely *bad ears* but Very Extremely *sharp eyes*. I think he might have infrared vision or something. Maybe he could team up with Tomato in a new smash hit Super Villain TV series.

So that was playtime spent in the head's office, writing lines. I had to think out something to say and I was quite pleased with it:

"Tongues are for talking and tasting, not for teachers."

But I felt a lot less pleased after writing it out fifty times. I'll tell you a secret, I wrote it out forty-six times. Then I wrote:

"Tongues are for teachers and tasting, not for talking."

Then I wrote it out properly twice more. So I did only forty-nine lines! Hah! And one of them was wrong! And Mrs Hedake didn't notice! Hah!

At the end of the day, we had three seriously good posters.

Here they are:

Mine: OK, I know I left the 'E' out of 'INCREDIBLE'. But I could tidy that up.

Chloe's: Huh. Harpo looks like LASSIE.

Dinah's: What?! Is Harpo in slippers?

Which would you choose?

Well, I hope you chose mine, because I hope you are a person of good taste and so on which is why you are reading this and not playing with Barbie.

But in fact, we chose this one:

Humph. My drawing was much better

Chapter 4

Another monster attack. This time, the monster spoke! "Hooray!" I said, waking blearily from my humble bed, Harpo was speaking to me! It wasn't all a dream!

"Tixie! Tixie!" said the monster. "Tixie! Bedallwet!"

Oh boo. It wasn't Harpo. It was Tomato. Why does he come into my bed and then have a little "accident". Why can't he have a little "accident" in his own nice dry bed?

And WHY won't Harpo speak to ME??

I spent all morning, well, the ten minutes between sorting Tomato out –"It's all right, Tom-Tom, accidents will happen, I'm the perfect sister who doesn't mind having to strip her bedclothes and comfort her little brother while her parents remain snoring dead to the world"– and breakfast, trying to get Harpo to talk but she just looked at me as if I was mad.

Right. It was definitely and Very Extremely important to check she won't do this on the Big Day. Imagine that excited audience, having paid big wads of fat money, and she won't pipe up!

Our household is not happy at the moment. Mum is still mooning about looking in every nook and cranny for her Diamond Togetherness Ring. She obviously feels superstitious about it, as though losing it is some Big Thing about her and Dad. This means she has nagged me and Tomato every day about tidying up, as she is sure we are responsible and that the ring will be found in a pillow, amid a pile of Duplo or something. She is probably right, but I have more things on my mind. I haven't dared mention my missing trumpet, let alone my Harpo fears.

At lunch time I got Dinah in a corner. I knew if I asked Chloe, she'd just call the whole thing off.

"Of course she'll do it on the day," Dinah said, with cheering confidence. "She always talks to me."

"I know," I said miserably. "But she has stopped talking to ME. Do you think she doesn't like me any more?"

"Of course not. It's just that you are like, well, her parent. You know, and she's kind of like, well, a sort of a teenager, and you know they never talk to their parents. Anyway, she doesn't need to impress you."

I knew Dinah was being nice, but I didn't want to be Harpo's mummy, really. I mean, I'm young and free, with my whole LIFE ahead of me. And I hated to think Harpo just took me for granted. So I tried Chloe. I knew I shouldn't have.

"Ish dishashtrusss," she said, thoughtfully, stuffing about six marshmallows in her mouth at once, and not offering me one.

"Eh what?"

"We can't (gobble gobble munch) posshibly..."

"Oh do stop talking with your mouth full," I snarled, and stomped off. I must say the sight of all those marshmallows not coming in my direction had a bad effect on my mood, which was not helped by Orange Orson who crept into the girls' loo and tried to stuff my head down it to make me give him my pound book token for book day. Orange Orson reading books!?

"Aieee! Lemmego!"

"G'iss your token!"

I suppose he thought he could sell it for fags. He's only eleven and he smokes already! I've seen him smoke three fags at once!!

Luckily, Mrs Hedake swarmed in at that very moment, on toilet patrol.

Unluckily she gave us both a detention at lunchtime.

I wonder if the man at the trumpet shop will count a World Book Day one pound token as real money?

You might wonder why I call my arch enemy Orange Orson; I bet you think he's got red hair. Wrong, hah, he has sort of beige hair.

I have this weird thing about colours. I see all the days of the week in colours, like Wednesday is Maroon and Thursday is Pink and Friday is Pea Green and Monday is Navy Blue.

Numbers as well: seven is Green, eight is Gold and so on. I like Purple best, I think it's a kind of wild colour – so my best friends are either Purple or Gold or Silver or maybe Blue or Red. And my enemies are all Orange or Grey.

Orson happens to have an 'O' name too, so it's lucky. And I hate Orange Orson about as much as anybody in school apart from Grey Griselda.

Grey Griselda, the tallest girl in the school, actually tripped over me on the way out of detention and said Very Extremely loudly to her witchily giggling friends: "Where are the birds when you need them? We've got a plague of worms." Then she looked down at me from her incredible towering height and said, "Oh no, silly me, it's a cockroach. Eeek! Call Pest Control!" Well, yah boo to Griselda. She looks like the Trifle Tower in France (which stays up pretty well without wobbling, considering, har har). I hope she enjoyed that hot chilli sauce I squeezed into her horrible-looking sandwich in her stupid old lunchbox with fairies on it.

But on the way home, I realised that neither of these Evil Enemies were as bad as the Terrible New Enemy that's come into my life. That weird old man who'd been on the bus the day I lost my trumpet was on the bus again.

He got off at the same stop as me, raised his stick as if he was going to put a spell on me with it, and started lurching towards me, saying something I couldn't hear. He was red in the face, and he had some teeth missing, and he was carrying a bulging supermarket bag. What was in it? Chopped-up children? Barbecued boys? Ghoulishly grilled girls?

I ran. He tried to run too, but luckily he couldn't keep up. I went the opposite way to my house, and lost him in the backstreets.

I got home shaking and out of breath. I needed comforting from someone who loves me.

No parents to be found, of course.

I went and looked for Harpo. Fast asleep, big surprise. But then Tomato came rolling down the stairs to greet me, and for a change I was really delighted to see him.

I really wanted to wake Harpo up, have a proper talk with her – remind myself that this wasn't a dream – and tell her about the old man and about my missing trumpet. Maybe she'll know what to do. But I mustn't tire her out. She has a big day coming. Maybe Dinah was right and Harpo needs a little space.

I decided to play it cool and let her come to me. That evening seemed to go very slowly.

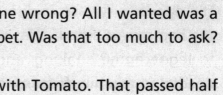

6 p.m.
Harpo asleep.
6.05 p.m.
She had still not spoken.
6.12 p.m.
Where had I gone wrong? All I wanted was a little chat with my pet. Was that too much to ask?
6.20 p.m.
I went to play with Tomato. That passed half

an hour quick as a wink. Play play play.

6.27 p.m.

Not a word from Harpo!

6.28 p.m.

"Tixshie play Buffaloes!" Buffaloes is Tomato's favourite game. We each hold a pillow in front of us and charge each other until one falls over. The one standing is the winning buffalo. You would think I would always win this game being so much older but no. But then you have not seen Tomato. Harpo was bound to notice what fun we were having and ask to join in.

6.35 p.m.

Time was doing that funny thing when you want it to behave differently. You know, how it always flies like it's got a rocket up its you-know-what when you're having fun, and potters along or just stands picking its nose when you're at the dentist, or doing evil Maths. Still nothing from Harpo.

6.36 p.m.

"Tomato," I asked. "Has Harpo said anything to you recently?"

"Harpo talk me all time," said Tomato smugly.

"Harpo tell me shecrets."

"What secrets?" I wasn't jealous. Honest.

"Shecrets," says Tomato, fiercely, as though I am lower than an ant. "Not shposed to tell shecrets. Notty Tixshie."

Oh, marvellous. My only little brother and my only pet against me. Can't wait till I get Merlin. And to think life seemed so good, so recently.

"More Buffaloes!" chanted Tomato, whacking me playfully with the biggest pillow.

"Ouch!" He had put some Duplo into the pillow. Was he going to grow up a vandal and add to my worries?

6.40 p.m.

The more I thought about Harpo snoozing all the time, the more I feared the show was going to be a disaster. These fears got bigger and bigger, and in the end I could barely concentrate on playing Buffaloes with Tomato, not that he noticed.

6.50 p.m.

I rang Chloe. "Have you finished your marshmallows? Good. Because I'm going to cancel *Harpo the Amazing Doggy Yap Star.*"

"Oh. OK," said Chloe. "But why are you ringing up in the middle of *Vera the Veggie Vampire?*"

I am really nuttyasafruitcake. I never miss *Vera the Veggie Vampire*. Now I'll have nothing to talk about to all those airheads in the playground who think *Vera the Veggie Vampire* is god.

Tomato and I turn it on to get the last three minutes, which is mostly credits. *Vera the Veggie Vampire* has the longest credits of any programme on earth, I swear it. They are all grisly pics of her murdering sprouts and escaping vast cabbages who are trying to drive stakes through her heart

74

and all, whatever. I wouldn't let kids my age watch it if *I* was in charge. Tomato doesn't mind it, even though his own meat-eating relatives come off pretty badly.

6.55 p.m.

I rang Dinah.

"Did you see *Vera the Veggie Vampire*?" she squawked down the phone before I could say anything after "Hi".

"Yeh, wasn't it great?" I said, hoping she wouldn't want to get into details.

"That carnivorous carrot!" she went on, enthusiastically. "And the attack of the blood-drinking broccoli!"

"Yeh," I went, drumming my fingers on the table.

Dinah, though she is an intelligent person, likes to go

through the plot in a way that I can only describe as, well, boring. And she tends to do all the voices. She will do a whole army of sweetcorn all with different accents unless you are Very Extremely firm with her. She does do a Very Extremely good Vera, you know that kind of American voice with a twang at the end that goes right through your head like a food blender.

I finally got a word in:

"I'm going to cancel *Harpo the Amazing Doggy Yap Star*."

"WHAT???!!"

That was more like it. That was what I was hoping for.

"You can't do that."

"I can."

"You can't."

"I can."

"You can't."

This went on for rather a long time but I don't want you all sneaking off to read fairy books, so the long and the short of it was, Dinah persuaded me to give Harpo another big rehearsal tomorrow (Friday) in preparation for her Specially Big Day on Sat.

"I know she can do it. I have a special relationship with her. It will be all right, honest. Think how brilliant she was only last night. And think of your folks and the trumpet and the *Save the World with a Song* concert."

And the old man on the bus, I thought to myself. Maybe I needed to pay somebody to save me from him.

Dinah convinced me, all over again.

Chapter 5

Sure enough, Friday evening after school, Harpo wouldn't speak.

I was there, Dinah was there, Chloe was there, we tried everything. We tried Fidoburgers in front of her nose. We tried pictures of Lorenzo. We begged and pleaded:

"Harpo, you can have a lifetime's supply of Lorenzo-lookalikes and Fidoburgers."

"You can have satin-lined baskets and never fetch the papers."

"I'll never make you run after a ball again. You can tell *me* to 'sit' and 'stay' and 'fetch'. I'll do anything you ask."

"You won't have to give pawtographs to your fans if you're not in the mood."

In desperation, I roped in Tomato, who, I hate to admit, seems to have a thing going with Harpo that I didn't have.

"Why not talkin' Harpo?" he asks her in his sweetest voice.

"Grw... fff," she muttered, wagging her tail for the first time that evening and licking strawberry jam off his nose. Maybe it's because he's always covered in something tasty that she likes him so much.

Tom-Tom put his ear close to Harpo's nose. "C'mon Harpo."

She nuzzled his ear. Was she whispering to him? Or licking this morning's breakfast off his sideburns? We were agog.

"Yush," said Tomato. "Yush yush, goodog Harpo." And with that, he rolled off in search of sweeties.

"Oh God. Oh God of Dogs, if there is one," I

said, hurling myself on my knees, "Give Harpo back her voice. I beg you. I will go to dog church, I will help starving dingos in Australia and give all Harpo's earnings to Battersea Dog's Home. I will feed the abused and neglected puppies of the world! But please, give Harpo back her voice."

I looked up. I had forgotten I was Not Alone. Dinah, Chloe and Harpo herself were all looking at me as if I was completely, well, barking mad.

"Well, why won't she **SPEAK?!**" I shouted, and stomped off over to the window to gaze at the gloomy rain falling mistily down on the gloomy rooftops.

"Lorenzo told me not to," said a doggie voice, unmistakably like Harpo.

"WHAT?!" I spun round, a small fragment of joy lighting my life.

"He doesn't want me to be an entertainer," said Harpo.

And with that she fell into one of her mega-deep sleeps.

"Oh no," said Dinah. "We have been selfish. Lorenzo is right. We just wanted to use Harpo's incredible talent to make money, but Lorenzo has her real best interests at heart."

"Yes," said Chloe.

I hate the way she does that. Just agrees with Dinah all the time.

"But what about the lost trumpet? What about my parents never speaking to me again **EVER!**" I cried.

"Tough turnips, Trixie," said Dinah. "I thought you believed in Animal Rights?"

If she hadn't said "Tough turnips", I might have agreed with her. But I just saw red.

"This is not a question of Animal Rights," I shouted. "This is a question of doing one little show!! Just for ME!! Who has fed and clothed that dog since she was the size of a chicken nugget?

"Who saved her from the streets and brought her up on kingsize Fidoburgers? And... and... EVERYTHING. She only has to do ONE LITTLE SHOW. THEN she can do whatever she WANTS!" And I whacked Dinah over the head with the nearest pillow. Unfortunately it was the pillow that Tomato had stuffed with Duplo. The resulting row seemed to wake Harpo. But obviously she had been listening all along, because she yawned and said,

"Yep." (Or was it "Yap"?)

"Oh Harpo," I shouted, "Will you? Will you really?"

"Yep."

"Yes! It was a definite Yes!"

Harpo could understand. Harpo *could* speak. Harpo *would* speak. It would be all right on the night!

We tiptoed out of my room and collided with my mum, who was bringing us up a tray of juice and biccies.

"You poor duck," squealed Mum when she saw Dinah. "How ever did you get a lump like that?"

I looked at Dinah's head. It was a bit alarming.

"Oh," stuttered Dinah. "Trixie and me were just... practising."

My mother looked bemused. "Practising what?"

"Oh, you know, headstands," said Chloe. Good old Chloe. Her caution always gives her time to think.

"And Dinah did hers on a pillow that was stuffed with DUPLO. WHO could've put THAT here?" I added.

"TOMATO!" yelled Mum. "I told you **NOT**

to stuff the pillows with Duplo. Look at poor Dinah."

Heh heh.

Can't sleep and we're due to meet up to plaster the town with posters at 6.45 a.m. tomorrow.

2.30 a.m.

Woke from scary dream. I was in a court and Harpo was the judge. She sat up on a big wooden thingy surrounded by a whole lot of other dogs in gowns and wigs. Two huge pit bull terriers pulled me onto another wooden thingy. And I realised I was the prisoner! But what was my crime?! I had no idea what I was there for! Then I saw a table marked EVIDENCE. And on it was my mum's Diamond Togetherness Ring. Surely I wasn't on trial for stealing my own mum's ring? You know how it is in dreams when you think you have done something bad? I was certain I had stolen the ring. But no. It was about something else...

Next thing, a vast chicken arrived carrying an enormous old book with ancient yellow pages, called LAW OF THE JUNGLE. The chicken flapped its wing over a few pages and then squawked with a mighty squawk and turned its tiny shiny eyes on me and said: "Did you, or did you not, seek to employ an entirely innocent animal for the purposes of making money for yourself and with no intention of paying the aforesaid innocent creature, namely, to whit, the noble and blameless citizen Harpo?"

"Well, yeh, but..."

"Answer only the question put to you!" stormed Harpo, bringing her little hammer down on the wooden thingy with a mighty thwack.

"Did you or did you not..."

"Objection!" quacked a small fat duck, who seemed to be on my side. "My client deeply regrets having exploited the aforesaid creature, and has since paid for Harpo to attend the best law school in the land."

"With what results?" asked the chicken, sarcastically.

"With the results, madam," quacked the duck happily, "that the aforesaid exploited creature became a judge, and is seated in this very court, judging my client as we quack."

"Objection overruled! Stuff and Nonsense! Rubbish and Balderdash! Baloney, bilge, bosh and bunk!" barked Harpo, betraying me. "Take her away and keep her in a cell so small she can neither stand nor sit, for sixteen days. Then roast her and bring her to me with sage and onion stuffing and a side portion of Fidoburgers. Court dismissed!"

There was uproar in the court, with all the dogs barking and wagging their tails and licking their lips, then the pit bulls leapt on me and I woke up sweating with Harpo on my head.

"Traitor," I muttered, but she didn't seem to care.

Help. Harpo's big day tomorrow. How would I go back to sleep now?

Chapter 6

8.45 a.m. Hah hah! We have put HARPO, THE AMAZING PERFORMING PET posters on every tree and lamppost in the neighbourhood. Luckily, Dinah's folks will not see these as they will be speeding by in a taxi in the opposite direction. Heh heh. Harpo told us yesterday that it would be of excellent goodness to choose trees and lampposts, because any other talking dogs in the neighbourhood would be sure to come. I hope she is not cracking up under the strain.

We had one dodgy moment when we spied Warty-Beak peering at one of the posters with his infrared gaze. Typical of Warty-Beak to be the only person up stretching his scales and sharpening his claws on a Saturday morning at 6.45 a.m. Maybe he's from a planet where nobody sleeps.

We froze when we saw him. Would he remember the butterfly life cycle thingy? Would he remember I pretended my caterpillar was called Harpo? Worse, would he TURN UP at Harpo's performance? Eek. He peered at the photo and then smiled. This was not a pretty sight. Dinah said we should kidnap him and lock him in a shed for the duration as she did not want his scaly claws on her mum's nice carpet.

"Nice carpet? We're going to have 500 kids on your mum's nice carpet!" It wasn't like Dinah to worry about a nice carpet.

"Yes. But five *thousand* children could not have the effect of one Warty-Beak claw," said Dinah. "Haven't you noticed, he leaves a slime trail, wherever he goes? And a strange smell, like overcooked sprouts?"

"Really?" said Chloe, eyes like flying saucers. For a clever person she is really stupid sometimes.

Then Dinah went home to break the news to

her sister Dora and get the house ready. If Dora gets difficult, Dinah was fully prepared to lure her into the attic and lock her in for the rest of the day. It's amazing that she was doing all this for me. She really is a True Friend.

Me and Chloe were going to shampoo and comb Harpo and maybe put a bow in her hair IF she didn't mind. Chloe was keen on giving her dreadlocks and a bow tie but I drew the line at that. She is a dog, after all, and deserves to run wild and free.

9.15 a.m.

Have you ever tried shampooing and blow drying a dog the size of a hippo that isn't keen on the idea? What was most annoying, was Harpo didn't say a thing. She just whined pathetically like any ordinary dog. I gave her a Fidoburger and two whole tins of deluxe Doggy Diner biccies.

"Careful," said Chloe predictably. "She's got to be able to walk about a bit to get to Dinah's."

I looked doubtfully at Harpo, who was looking Very Extremely grumpy indeed and, it is true, about twice her usual size. This was partly owing to the Very Extremely electric look her fur gets if you blow dry it.

"She looks like a porcupine in a hurricane," said Chloe cheerfully. "I told you we should use conditioner."

"Look Harpo," I wheedled, "just say if you don't want the bow, all right? I won't put the bow on if you don't want it."

"Grwffff."

"You ARE going to talk at the show, aren't you."

"Grwwwff."

"That's yes, I suppose," said Chloe doubtfully.

"Course it is," I said, taking Harpo and my courage in both arms and giving her the biggest hug in the world. She squeaked rather alarmingly and hauled herself up onto my bed and started circling.

"That's right, have a nice nap and you'll feel much better. Get your strength up for the Big Event," I said, as cheerfully as I could. And off I went with Chloe.

"I have a feeling this isn't going to work out," she said. "Which isn't like me."

"Oh yes, it is like you. It's more like you are than you are."

"What's that supposed to mean?" asked Chloe, looking hurt.

"Oh shut up," I responded wittily, engulfed, by now, in Very Extremely deep gloom. Would everyone laugh at my beloved hippo-porcupine? Would she say anything except Bark and Woof?

Noon:

We had it all sorted! And the show didn't even start till six! We are brilliant! Dinah's humungously huge front room looked absolutely extremely amazing. We stood the immense ping-pong table from Dinah's garage (which in itself is a good bit bigger than my whole house) on big fat serious-looking books from Dinah's mum's immense library to make a stage. And we took every chair, stool, box and cushion in the whole place, and decided seated audiences could pay £1, everybody else 50p.

And this will be only the first of Harpo's many amazing performances!

The refreshments were dead easy: we got loads of Very Extremely cheap orange drink and some rock cakes that Mrs Dough the baker gave us for nothing because they are four days after their sell-by date, but with rock cakes it doesn't make much difference.

The only teensy snag was that Dinah hadn't been able to persuade her sister Dora that any of this was a good idea. She hadn't been able to persuade her into the attic either, but nabbed her by the devilish trick of hiding Dora's mobile phone in the snooker room (YES! They have a snooker room!), ringing it up and then locking her in there when she went to look for it. The house is so big you could only just hear Dora moaning and banging and carrying on from where the Big Show was going to be, and we reckoned once it was full of audience all chattering and cheering, nobody would hear her at all. I didn't ask Dinah

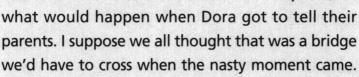

what would happen when Dora got to tell their parents. I suppose we all thought that was a bridge we'd have to cross when the nasty moment came.

It all seemed to be going just great. Tiddley um pom pom. TIDDLEY POM, I thought.

1 p.m.

You are not going to believe this. We had got everything together, it all looked wonderful. But JUST the eggzact minute I was thinking Tiddley Pom, a terrible terrible thing happened.

Harpo disappeared.

I don't mean she vanished like a conjuror's assistant, no, nothing clever like that. No. She

Went Missing. I came straight home after we'd sorted out about Dinah's house and ran up to give Harpo a cuddle and talk her through her schedule. There was a large Harpo-shaped patch on my bed. But Harpo wasn't in it.

"Tom-Tom, have you got Harpo in there?" I shouted through the bathroom door.

Harpo quite often has a bath with Tomato (even though getting her to have a bath on her own is a job for five strong men).

"No. Nottydog. Play Buffaloes?"

"Where is she then?'

"Not seen Harpo. Notty dog."

Oh woe woe woe woe is me. My poor pet has gone. I have scared her away with talk of fame and fortune. She has spurned the dazzling lights of Collywood and has gone to be an ordinary dog somewhere, alone. Or maybe not... **OF COURSE**, she has gone Next-Door to live with Lorenzo!

Be prepared, some of this story is Sad from now on.

After I had the absolutely extremely certain brainwave that Harpo had gone to seek comfort from Lorenzo, I charged straight next door.

Mrs Next-Door, who has a face like a sackful of ferrets and a temper to match, opened the door one centimetre on a chain.

"Oh, it's you," she grimaced, reluctantly releasing the 400 locks and bolts bristling all over her porch. I can't see what a burglar would find to take in their house. It's all full of extremely horrible jugs and vases with no flowers in. What's the point of hundreds an' hundreds of horrible empty vases that a child or a dog is just bound to knock over? Lorenzo must have such a sad life.

"Have you seen Harpo?" I blurted.

"Not since I shooed her off yesterday. She does upset poor Lorenzo so."

At this point smarmy, handsome old Lorenzo came lolloping up and covered Mrs Next-Door in slobbery kisses. Some dogs have absolutely no taste in humans whatever.

"There there, ickle petty. Duzzoooo want a

biccy?" smirked Mrs Next-Door, more or less shutting the door in my face.

But by now I was panicking. Harpo was not with Lorenzo. Harpo was missing. Truly.

I phoned Dinah and Chloe and they hurtled round. We formed a search party and, of course, Tomato had to join in. And then soppy Poppy from over the road – she's a sad, pale child who I'm sorry to say always reminds me of Cheesy Strings. And then Bugsy and Wax, the mad twins from the flats, poled up. So we were quite a team really and my spirits rose. Surely, between us, we could track down Harpo?

"You mean that big fat dog the size of an elephant?" said Wax. "I seen her in the lift."

So we charged over to the flats and hurtled into the lift in a big wodge. Er. Why were we all in the lift, when all we had to do was look in the lift to see if Harpo was in there? Because that's the sort of thing you do when you aren't thinking, OK?

Of course soppy Poppy had pressed the button by the time yours truly had had the above amazing thought, so we were trundling up to the tenth floor.

96

"We got to press all the buttons in case she got out," said Wax. So we did. Not on floor one. Not on floor two. I won't go on. We ran up and down all the corridors of all the flats shouting and knocking and calling Harpo.

Burly Bert the hairdresser came rocketing out on floor ten and said he was sure he'd seen Harpo down the burger bar.

"Why would she go there?" asked soppy Poppy.

We all looked at Poppy and she went redder than Tomato.

"Perhaps Harpo was trying to buy a hot dog," suggested Dinah kindly.

"Nah. She's probly down the takeaway getting a couple of Puppadoms," said Wax.

I thought I'd die laughing. Not. "This is no time for stupid jokes," I wailed.

We raced off to the burger bar. No sign of Harpo.

"You mean that dog what looks like a polar bear on steroids?" said the bloke at the till.

"Yeh. Yeh."

"So big it can hardly move?"

"YES!!!"

"No, I ain't seen it."

"What do you mean? You just described her!"

"Well I seen it come out for the paper most days, don't I?"

We charged up the road to the newsagent's, all of us ignoring the notice that said: "No more than two schoolchildren at a time."

Mr Drugg was not amused at the sight of seven children storming his shop. **"OUT,"** he shouted, politely. Luckily Mr Drugg caught sight of me waving my tiny arm amid the throng. "Oh, Trixie. They all with you?"

OUT!

"Yes, Mr Drugg," I said in my best extremely polite tones. "We're looking for Harpo. She's gone missing."

"Harpo? But she was in here this morning as usual," he said, a worried frown creasing his friendly mug. Drugg's mug is friendly, except when he's on the warpath against hundreds of children stealing penny sweeties.

"I know," I said, feeling my lip trembling in an extremely worrying way. "And then I gave her a bath and stuff and she just upped and disappeared!"

"Well, she can't have got very far," he said reassuringly. "You know, being so fat."

I felt sadder than ever when he said that. I have always thought of Harpo as cuddly. But now here was even her friend, Mr Drugg, saying that she was a heffalump. I have not been looking after my pet properly, I thought. I have only wanted to use her for my own selfish ends. I have been feeding her too much, to try to get her to love me and talk to me and now she has rejected me by running away. Except she is too fat to run and has probably been knocked down by a ten-ton truck and is lying breathing her last on some remote highway, as in fact she might have been missing for **THREE WHOLE HOURS** which is when I last saw her. Well, this is the sort of thing that was going through my head, I can tell you. And I bet if you have any kind of heart at all it would've been going through yours, too.

"HEY! THERE she is!" shouted Dinah, pointing wildly at a furry blur lolloping down the road. We all galloped after her, but then—

"LOOK!" said Chloe, eyes like cups and saucers. I looked.

We all looked.

Every lamppost in the High Street proudly displayed the posters we had pasted up. They were pretty impressive. But there was one little, no, *enormous* difference. Every poster had been altered to say: ...*And the amazing performing pets. Bring your own pet! Big prizes!*

"This means trouble, big time. Your house will be full of animals," was Chloe's cheerful response.

"We better get to my place quick," said Dinah.

"What about Harpo?" I cried.

But they had hared off and I was left holding a sobbing Tomato, "Where Harpo? Harpo dead!" and a sopping Poppy, while gazing at the baffled faces of Wax and Bugsy.

"You mean that big lump of lard we're lookin' for is a *talkin'* dog?" said Wax.

"She's not a lump of lard."

"Nottywaxy. Shootimded," said Tomato valiantly.

"Hey, that means we gotta find him," said Bugsy. "We'll get a reward!"

"He's not a HE. He's a SHE," I said, as Wax and Bugsy charged off in the vague direction of the furry blur.

"I've got an idea," said soppy Poppy.

I nearly fainted. It was quite surprising she should actually have a whole idea of her own. I stared, trying to hold back the tears. Tomato stared.

"When my cat went missing," said soppy Poppy, Very Extremely slowly in a little voice like a vole, "we found her..."

"YES YES, WHERE?" I shouted.

"...in her basket."

"Oh. Great."

"I know it sounds silly," said Poppy, blushing so that she turned from Irish Cheddar yellow to Red Leicester pink, "but animals often return to where they are I... I... loved."

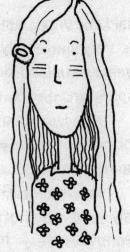

An arrow, so to speak, pierced my heart. Was Harpo loved? Or exploited for evil money?

Then I heard a triumphant shout from the top of a bus. "We've got her!"

I looked up to see Wax and Bugsy falling off the bus platform clutching the furry blur. It was a big dog certainly, but nothing at all like Harpo.

"That's not her!"

"Well, it looks exactly like her," said Wax, gazing at Dinah's poster. I didn't like to admit that it did look Very Extremely like Dinah's stupid old drawing.

"Thief! DOG THIEF!" came a furious shout. At which point the furry blur launched itself into the loving arms of its enraged owner, a grim-looking woman the size of a van. Wax sped off like lightning, leaving yours truly to explain. Luckily, the posters were a help.

"Oh you poor darling, lost your little pet,"

said the woman surprisingly kindly. Sometimes it is Very Extremely excellent, looking about six years old, like I do, especially when you have a spherical, scarlet, weeping brother in your arms.

"I DO hope you find her, and perhaps I shall bring Romulus along. He's awfully good at somersaults."

I thought quickly. I turned to Bugsy and said, my heart lifting: "Right. Me and Tomato and Poppy are going home. I'm sure you're right, and that Harpo will be there. Meanwhile, if you lot could go on looking, just in case, I'll give you a BIG reward if you find her."

I trailed home with a furious making-such-a-noise Tomato – "Wantfindnottydog. Killwaxded. Shootbangbangbang" – I was tempted to abandon him in case someone called the social services and accused me of heartless brutality. But then I thought leaving him would be even worse and I'd probably get sent to prison for life or something. Mind you, prison would probably be the safest place for me once the Audience finds out there isn't a Talking Dog at all. And Dinah's sister gets out of that snooker room, and Dinah's parents get home. And my parents not only find out about all that but find out my trumpet's gone as well.

We went round the corner to my street... and there he was again.

The old man. Right in front of us. Face redder than ever, and I'm sure he was missing more teeth than usual as he opened his horrible, twisted mouth to shout: "YOU!!"

He was struggling to get something out of his bag. Was it a knife, or a gun? Or a big net, to catch us all in, and drag us away to whatever cave or hollow tree or haunted house or hole in the ground he lived in?

I grabbed Tomato and Poppy by the back of their T-shirts. And yanked them round and ran across the road, just missing a bus, which hooted at us. It came between us and the old man, and when it had gone by we hid behind a parked car. He was looking round for us, but didn't see us. Crawling from car to car, we somehow made our way home.

When I got in, I needed Harpo more than ever. If she was there, fast asleep on my bed as though

104

nothing had happened, I would cancel the show and all our plans for her and everything, and just hug her and tell her she needn't talk to anybody ever again if she didn't want to.

But she wasn't there.

There was nothing on my bed except the flattened Harpo area I hadn't touched since she disappeared. I put a note on it, saying "DO NOT DISTURB". It might be the last sign I ever saw of her...

Chapter 7

MEANWHILE...

I know you can't wait to know what happened to Harpo, but I have to fill you in on the horrible scenes that awaited Dinah and Chloe when they got to Dinah's house.

I didn't get to hear the horrible details until they told me later, of course. I was still weeping on my Harpoless bed. But apparently there was a queue outside about a mile long of kids and pets of all ages and sizes, all hoping to win Big Prizes.

Poor Dinah had to announce that there wasn't going to be a Doggy Yap Star after all, but after a few boos and hisses, people apparently took it pretty well, considering. They were more interested in their own pets than somebody else's, whether it could talk or not – and Dinah reckoned half the pet-carrying people there probably believed their pets talked to them anyway, the loonies.

Everybody agreed it would be better to have a Performing Pet show than nothing at all. And so they started letting everyone in! And, even better, they all started to hand over their money!

Guess who was first? Orange Orson with two racing slugs! Eurgh. I bet it was him that changed the posters. Guess who was next? Grey Griselda with a PARROT!

Guess who was NEXT?

No, really, it was... it was...WARTY-BEAK.

I'll tell you about his pet in a minute. I was still at home begging Mum to ring the police, the vet, the social services, the secret services and the army to FIND Harpo.

Wax rang up to say he had her. He turned up with a puppy the size of an egg cup. I ask you!

Bugsy rang to say he'd seen her in the garden of number FORTY-ONE. I raced over, banged on the door, got no answer, climbed the fence, fell onto their greenhouse, smashed it, cut my leg and found... a goat. It's amazing what people keep in their gardens these days.

As Mum was bandaging my leg, I heard a little, unmistakably Harpo-like moan. It was coming from the garden.

I'd never moved so fast in my life. There was more moaning, then a bit of scratching. Harpo had obviously got in to my mother's shed. Why hadn't I looked in there before? Because my mother's shed is not a place that me or Harpo or Tomato are ever allowed into. It is a place where she does embarrassing things like write poems and plant little rare plants that wave one scrawny leaf in the breeze as if saying goodbye before curling up and dying. But somehow Harpo had got in, and obviously couldn't get out again.

"Oh Harpo, Harpo, Harpo," I cried, happy as I had ever been. Happier.

I couldn't budge the door, but Tomato just pulled it off its hinges and there was Harpo in among the poems and little dead green things, panting and wagging her tail like a loony.

"Oh Harpo. Have you been here all day?" I asked.

"Grwffff," she said happily.

"Oh I love you," I said, hugging my big enormous fat brillo pillow, fluff mountain, fur barrel, dog-of-my-dreams.

"Grwff," she replied

I didn't care about the show any more, but I had to let Dinah and Chloe know Harpo was all right. Tomato and I hauled her into the wheelbarrow and I set off to Dinah's house at about twice the speed of light. Dinah was in the front drive, trying to help a yelling toddler catch a very cross-looking and surprisingly fast-moving hedgehog.

"Harpo! Fantastic! The show can go on!" shouted Dinah, as soon as she saw us. She can be a little bit selfish at times.

"NO, she isn't well," I said, keen to defend my pet. I had had enough of worrying about the money. I could clean cars and do a paper round all year to get a trumpet. "She needs the vet," I said in my firmest voice. "She's been in the shed all day. She's very stressed and exhausted."

"Grwff," said Harpo happily, leaping about in the wheelbarrow, or as near to leaping as she could manage.

"Rubbish. She's fine," said Dinah briskly.

"Look," I said, "she's lost her voice anyway. She's got a sore throat. She hasn't said anything but 'Grwfff' to me."

"Nothing new there then," said Dinah meanly.

"Well, let's ask Harpo what she thinks," said Chloe, clutching another small child who was trying to extract a vast worm from its trouser pocket without pulling it in half.

"She won't talk! I'm in charge," I said, furiously.

"Nonsense." I heard a gruff Harpo voice. "Of

course I'll do the show, I'd hate to disappoint my fans."

"Attagirl Harpo," cried Dinah.

I was gobsmacked. "But she really isn't well. Look how she's panting," I said.

"We'll carry her then," said Dinah.

So we did. Me and Chloe and Dinah carried ten-ton Harpo over the fence into Dinah's garden so that her arrival wouldn't be seen by the Audience milling around in the front room. It was hard work trundling Harpo through hedges, around ornamental ponds full of scary fish, and up the back path. Unfortunately we brought down a big line of washing which sadly fell into one of the water features Mrs Dare-deVille is so fond of. When we finally burst through the French windows we found ourselves amid chaos.

About a hundred kids were shouting "WHY ARE WE WAITING?" Dogs were chasing cats, cats were chasing rats, two parrots and a budgie had taken refuge in the lampshades, and there were about eight hamsters, assorted rabbits and a couple of goldfish bowls. Performing goldfish?! I ask you. Oh, yeah, the goat was there too. And a sheep. And a goose. And a ferret. The area where I live is full of Very Extremely odd people, obviously.

A tall thin girl I didn't know was standing on a chair in the middle of the room screaming like a fruit bat, "GETTITOUT, GETTITOUT, GETTITOUT!"

"It's only a mouse!" snarled Orson Orange.

"It's not the mouse!" squealed the tall thin girl. "The mouse has been eaten. Look!"

Everybody looked.

A large snake with a lump in its middle was slithering gracefully towards the tall thin girl's chair. Even Orson Orange froze.

"It's eaten Jaws!" squealed a small boy the size of a peanut. "It's eaten my Singin' Mouse! That mouse was worth a billion pounds!"

"That is not your Singing Mouse, that is a perfectly dead and suitably nutritious defrosted mouse provided by me," said a strangely familiar cackling voice. The owner of the voice – I bet you've guessed who it was – now loomed into view, holding a Very Extremely ordinary-looking and perfectly alive mouse which he deposited in the hands of the little boy. "I am sorry to

disappoint you by returning your mouse instead of a billion pounds in compensation. Now come here Tiddles, don't be silly." The snake immediately stopped its pursuit of the gibbering girl on the chair and turned to slide into the loving arms of Warty-Beak!

Tiddles curled itself happily round Warty-Beak's neck – two reptiles happy together at last. And Warty-Beak immediately started behaving like a teacher. "Right, since I gather the star performer has now arrived, I think we can begin the show. Shall I be announcer?" He glanced at Dinah.

"Oh. Yes, PLEASE!" said Dinah. "I don't think Harpo is quite ready to perform yet."

"No. SHE is the STAR, after all," sneered Warty-Beak. "She must be the CLIMAX, the TOP-OF-THE-BILL. She is, after all, a TALKING DOG. Heh heh heh."

I looked at Harpo, who looked as if she had been pulled through a hedge backwards, which of course she had. She was also panting alarmingly and whimpering. I hugged her and hauled her behind the curtains to tidy her up a bit, while Warty-Beak continued to torture the crowd. The advantage of him being there, was that everyone had quietened down, as they sometimes do, with really scary teachers.

"I think we should hear the Singing Mouse first," sniggered Warty.

Peanut boy shambled on to the stage, held out his hand with the mouse on it and squeaked: "Afternoon ladles and jellyspoons! I am proud to present to yoooo, all the way from RodentVille, specially for your Hentertainment today – Jaws, the world's one and only Singin' Mouse."

Everybody cheered.

Silence.

"Come on, Jaws," said peanut boy. "Gissa tune."

"Eeek," squeaked Jaws.

"Wossat?" said peanut boy.

"Eeeek."

"Hey. This isn't Jaws. Your snake 'as ate 'im."

Clearly peanut boy did not know Warty-Beak was a teacher. Or else he was braver than you and me, dear reader.

Tiddles reared up alarmingly over Warty's head, hissing.

Everyone screamed.

Peanut boy, who will go far in life, just sauntered offstage. "I'll get my dad onto you," he said, waving a fist in Warty's direction. "That mouse was worth a billion pounds."

Everybody cheered again.

"This is great!" said Dinah. "Everyone's having a really good time."

"It's a disaster," said Chloe. "Look at the state of your mum's room. And look at Harpo."

Harpo was, of course, asleep.

"Oh, she's just having a refreshing nap," said Dinah. "She'll be fine."

The next act was Orange Orson and his racing slugs. He put a bit of lettuce down and put the slugs about two inches away from it. "I am betting that this one will win. Does anyone here agree to give me five pence if it does?"

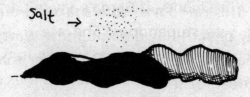

Salt →

The last few seconds in the life cycle of a slug...

A large number of small children agreed. Orson then poured salt on the other slug, which melted horribly in front of the poor little things disgusted eyes!

"Yeurgh. That's cheatin'! That's horrible!"

I marched onstage. "Get off, Orson," I shouted.

Everybody cheered.

"Now, has anyone got a REAL performing pet instead of this old rubbish?" I asked.

And so we saw Gerda the Greedy Goat.

"My goat will eat ANYTHING," said its proud owner, who was of course, the girl from number forty-one. "And I got to make some money 'cos my mum will kill me if she finds out Gerda smashed our greenhouse."

"Oh, that's terrible!" I said, thinking quicker than forked lightning. "I'll give you um, some of the box office money, if Gerda's any good."

Gerda was stupendous. She ate a glove, a peanut butter sandwich, two woolly hats and a small sweatshirt. Then she started on the curtains and Dinah had to haul her off.

"How about one of the goldfish?" I asked, 'cos

I don't mind telling you, I couldn't begin to think what a goldfish might do in the way of performing. So that was how I got to present Lily Arbuckle and Galadriel the Geometric Goldfish.

Lily, who was a Very Extremely tall girl with a Very Extremely small head that looked as though it had originally belonged to a much younger child, came proudly on stage carefully carrying her little bowl of treasure.

"This is the most amazing goldfish in the world," said Lily. "She can add and subtract. Watch her tail carefully."

We craned our necks.

"What is two add two?" said Lily.

I swear it, the goldfish's tail waved four times!

"What is four minus three?" said Lily.

Galadriel waved her tail once!

I KID YOU NOT!

"How many sides has a triangle?"

THREE WAVES!!

Then a horrible thing happened. Tabitha the Tortoiseshell Tap-dancer, who had run up the curtains to escape Gerda the Greedy Goat, plummeted from the pelmet in a leopard-like pounce, straight into Galadriel's bowl! Galadriel gasped her last. Lily was escorted weeping from the stage.

Enough is enough. "We have already lost a slug and a goldfish," I cried. "This is supposed to be a pet show, not a slaughterhouse. It is time for the star of the show! Er... Chloe will announce her." And I scurried behind the curtains, my heart in my mouth as they say, to wake up Harpo.

She was wide awake as it happened, and panting like a steam engine. She waved her tail weakly at the sight of me.

"Come on, Harpo, this is your big moment," I whispered, pushing her gently towards the stage.

Chloe did an impressive drum roll on biscuit tins.

"And now, the moment you've all been waiting for! The Pooch with the Patter! The Conversing Canine! Introducing the one and only Harpo, the AMAZING DOGGY YAP STAR," said Dinah.

Everybody cheered.

I gave Harpo another shove and she hurtled on stage unfortunately knocking Dinah onto a small squashy toddler in the front row.

Trembling, I could only think of my first, memorable conversation with Harpo:

"What's on top of a house?" I asked.

"Woof."

"Yes, that's right. Roof. OK Harpo, now what are trees made of?"

"BARK," went Harpo.

Then I asked her whether bark is smooth or rough.

"RUFF," went Harpo, sounding like any other dog in town.

Everyone booed. A couple of people (Orange Orson and Grey Griselda, naturally,) threw tomatoes. WHAT?! They brought a whole bag. They were handing them out!

Desperately, I shouted, "What rhymes with towel?"

"Growl," went Harpo.

"She's just warming up," I cried, fending off a tomato the size of, well, Tomato himself.

"She can sing, can't you Harpo?" I wailed, above the jeers. "Come on, give us your Top Ten."

"Yap, Yap Gruffitty Yap, Grrrrrr. Waooooow..."

My mind went blank, totally. I looked round frantically for Dinah, but she was distracted by two things: soothing the squashed toddler and attempting to disentangle herself from a large orange and blue parrot that had decided to stand on her head, make a very realistic whistling sound, and shout, "Offside!"

By then Harpo was circling and panting and making Very Extremely strange noises indeed.

The booing was getting louder and louder –
Very Extremely loud indeed. The tomatoes kept
coming. Splat. Sploing. Spludge.
"Wait," I stammered, desperately.
"She really CAN talk."

Then came an even more
ferociously loud sound even
than the audience or the
animals: "WHAT THE
HELL IS GOING ON
HERE?"

"Wicked," said Orson, impressed. "But what's
she sayin'?"

But it was *not* Harpo speaking. I was struck
dumb. So was Dinah. So was Chloe. So was
everyone else. Even the tomatoes stopped in
mid air.

We all looked round, horrified. It was Dinah's
dad, even redder in the face than Tomato, with
Dinah's mum close behind looking as if she was
about to faint – and smug-looking doomy Dora
behind them. She caught Dinah's eye with a very
horrible smile, and slowly waved the mobile
phone in the air.

Nobody knew what to say. Even Dinah's Dad seemed a bit at a loss after that outburst, as he took in the very strange scene around him.

The only living thing that did have something to say, was Harpo.

Because Harpo let out the most tremendously loud yelp. Then she lay down and groaned.

"That dog is not going to talk," said Warty-Beak, "that dog's having puppies."

And it's true. She was.

Chapter 8

HARPO HAD FIVE PUPPIES.

Two looked exactly like her. Two looked exactly like – guess who? – Lorenzo. And one had a sort of Harpo-ish, Lorenzo-ish face. I called him Bonzo. He was the most Very Extremely sweetest puppy you have ever seen ever in your life, ever. If you could think of the sweetest thing in the world, and I'm not talking marshmallows or strawberry ice cream, remember, I'm talking extremely serious cuteness, then you would choose Bonzo, I think. He would win the

Universe's Nicest Thing prize. I am absolutely one hundred percent determined to keep him. But it will take some doing for the following reasons.

The Dare-deVilles were, of course, not impressed by the state of their house when they returned and the distraction of Harpo giving birth in the middle of their dramatic arrival didn't keep them off the subject of going on and on at all and sundry about it for long.

I didn't know how a cheese sandwich got wedged in their CD player, or how the sink got blocked up with what looked like a dead porcupine (but fortunately wasn't – I didn't want another murdered animal on my conscience). I also could not explain how the fridge door came off or why the bath was full of chicken feathers.

As I have told my parents many times in the last few hours, there were certainly no chickens present. Budgies, yes – and parrots, but no chickens. For all I know, Dora is a secret chicken sacrificer and maybe the Dare-deVilles should look more closely at their own family's habits before blaming EVERYTHING on me.

I also couldn't explain who it was that ate the special birthday cake and forty-eight cocktail sausages that were in the fridge. The goat just ate clothing and never got near the kitchen as far as I could see. But as I said to Mum and Dad, several times, with a dodgy door like that, someone, probably a squirrel, could've easily got in and nicked everything. Although squirrels and goats are, as far as I know, sensible veggy type animals and would turn their snouts up at cocktail sausages.

But that was the least of it.

There were things I had to admit had not gone as well as they might: the shredded curtains (Tabitha); the large number of squashed tomatoes (several of them in the video machine and one, rather sadly, all over a hand-crocheted cushion cover that Mr Dare-deVille's great-great-great-grandmother made while she was awaiting execution in the French revolution or something); the melted slug remains; the smashed goldfish bowl with its sad little wet castle, that had been the last earthly home of poor little Galadriel; the budgie feathers; the rabbit and gerbil poo (some people have no idea how to look after their pets); the small lake of orange juice (this was when the goat barged past the drinks' table which wasn't exactly my fault, but...) and the Very Extremely amazingly huge amount of Very Extremely muddy footprints, which I blame on children who don't know they should always take their shoes off when entering a strange living room.

And living rooms don't come much stranger than the Dare-deVilles, at least not after the Great Performing Pet Experience.

As a matter of real actual fact, I couldn't believe that Mrs Dare-deVille had been stupid enough to leave out that old crocheted cover for the general public if it was so special, although I admit I wish I hadn't used it to mop up the juice and slug bits. It looked just like an old tomato-covered dishcloth to me.

So you see I was in what Grandma Clump calls "BAD BOOKS". If Grandma Tempest was here, she would say: "Nonsense, just childish pranks. She wants to keep the puppy? Of course she should! And she must be given an army of toads, witchy cats and palomino stallions too, for she has seventeen generations of witchy blood coursing through her veins!" At least, I think that's what she would say. But in the meantime I was in my room, where I had to stay until I had felt sorry for all my sins and had worked out several "I am sorry for all my sins" letters.

These were not just to each member of the Dare-deVille family by the way. I also had to write letters to:

1) toddler who fell into the Dare-deVille's ornamental stream while chasing the Grand Prix hedgehog and has had a cold ever since. I don't think this toddler can read yet, but I'm supposed to write to it anyway.

2) toddler's mum, and also to other toddler's mum who was persuaded by Persons Unknown (probably Wax and Bugsy) to fry his worm in the Dare-deVille's million pound French chef's special frying pan and eat it. Eating it apparently didn't do him any harm, but his parents think he may now need a child psychiatrist to get over having eaten his own pet.

3) Mrs Boot at number forty-one (greenhouse). Well, my better nature made me admit I broke it, because I didn't want the nice girl with the goat to get into trouble (she's called Sonya Boot, so I have to feel sorry for her really. Well you would, wouldn't you?)

4) Lily Arbuckle, promising to get her a new goldfish. I sussed out how she did that Very Extremely stupid trick. She just asks the questions very quickly as the fish is waving its tail. She just counts the right number of tail waves and then shoots in quickly with another question. The fish is in fact just waving its tail about all the time, because that's what goldfish DO. But everyone is so busy listening to the question and then counting the tail waves, nobody notices! I'm

amazed someone as clever as me was taken in by such a cheap trick, ahem. Good idea though. I think I might try it, as Harpo is going to be too busy being a mum to give a performance for a bit.

5) **Warty-Beak, apologising for fake butterfly cycle thingy and not giving his snake a chance to do its trick.** I expect it involved wrapping itself round small children till they breathed their last, but Mum said it was very rude not giving a teacher a go. Hah!

6) **soppy Poppy's mum, who had to shave quite a lot of Poppy's hair off in order to remove whatever it was Tomato had stuck to Poppy's nut.** He said it was just chewing gum, but I Have My Doubts.

7) Tortoisehell Tabitha's owners for the expense of the fire brigade getting her out of the tree and so on and on.

Another Very Extremely bad thing: our parents have made us give all the money back.

The worst thing of all the Very Extremely bad things that have happened to me, is that the *Save the World with a Song* concert is on Saturday week, and after everything that's happened already I just haven't been able to summon up the courage to tell my Mum and Dad about the trumpet too. The Diamond Togetherness Ring still hasn't shown up, and with all this stuff coming on top of it, they look just about at the end of their tether, whatever that is.

I may have to end up doing the thing I said I would never do for anybody or anything. I may have to give up my Merlin fund, which would be a drop in the ocean compared to what I've done, and would also be the end of all my dreams, but there comes a time, as some old movie says, when you just have to Do The Right Thing.

But to make it all worser still, Harpo is not talking to me AT ALL. She does not even notice me. She was bright as a button and slim as a ferret the minute she had her puppies and now all she thinks about is them.

She and Tomato were sitting drooling over them while I was forced to write millions of "I am sorry for all my sins" letters.

But WAIT. What was that? The doorbell!

It was Chloe and Dinah, my two best friends in all the world.

My mum wouldn't let them in at first, because my punishment was supposed to be not to see anybody outside the family until all my letters were written and I've repented for all my sins. But they told her it was all their fault as much as mine and since their parents had relented a bit and let them go out, Mum didn't have the heart to keep it up.

They also told her that all the kids' parents had said we could keep the money in the end because THE AMAZING PERFORMING PET SHOW was so extremely amazing and it was Very Extremely educational for the kids to see such a lovely litter of puppies born. And wasn't it nice that kids today are doing real things with their pets instead of just watching videos and playing computer games?

Dinah's Mum and Dad, who turned out to be Really Safe in the end, had even seen the funny side and said that the damage wasn't really that bad and wouldn't make much difference to their bank account, which I'm sure is absolutely true but nice of them anyway.

It was Very Extremely lucky that no one mentioned the dead goldfish or the salted slug. We kids stick together when it matters. Dinah also never told her parents what the Show had really been raising money for, for which I was Very Extremely glad, even though the truth was very near to coming out now. They thought we'd been raising money for endangered species, which probably helped the fuss to blow over a lot.

Mum unruffled her feathers a bit when she heard what all the parents had said: "Well. It's very kind of them I'm sure and at least the money can help to repaint Dinah's living room and get some new curtains."

Oh. Great.

But she did let Dinah and Chloe upstairs to join me in my room-of-pain. And that is when the most surprising thing of all happened.

"How is Harpokins?" asked Dinah, a rather funny look on her mug, I thought.

"OK," I said.

"Can't we see her? And the puppykins?"

I hate it when Dinah goes all soppy like that.

We sloped off to visit Harpo. Tomato was fast asleep on top of her, with a puppy in each of his four pockets and one on his head.

"Ooooooooooooh, so sweeeeet," cooed Dinah and I didn't mind, because it was.

"Hello Harpo," said Dinah.

"Oh, Hi, Dinah, Hi, Chloe," said Harpo. "Hi, Trix," she added, as an afterthought.

"That's the first time she's spoken since we were in Mum's shed!" I shouted. "Harpo, I know you were having puppies and all that at the show. But why do you never speak when we're alone?" I cried, cuddling her enormous head.

"Because I can't," said Harpo.

"What do you mean?"

"I can't talk to you when we're alone."

"WHY NOT?"

"Because I can't talk," said Harpo.

"WHAAAAAT? You just did!"

"It's not me," said Harpo.

I was Very Extremely annoyed by this time.

"What do you mean, it's not you?"

"It never was me. It was Dinah."

Well, I expect the very clever readers among you, who have never opened a comic in their life and probably read Shakespeare for fun and are grade eight on the cello or something, will have guessed this long before and think I am Very Extremely unbelievably stupid for not guessing. But that's how it is, sometimes. You have a friend who is the most brilliant mimic in the school and possibly the world, and you have a dog that starts talking. The dog only talks when your friend is there. But you don't put two and two together. Or at least, yours truly, dumb-dumb of the year, didn't.

Of course, I wanted to kill Dinah immediately and the ensuing fight woke up Tomato and all the puppies, so it got a bit noisy. Luckily Chloe managed to wedge herself between us before I did too much damage.

"Did YOU know?" I rounded on Chloe, who was holding both my arms in a vice-like grip. She is stronger than she looks, Chloe.

"No. Not till half an hour ago."

This made me feel a little teeny bit better.

"I'm sorry Trix, I really am. It started as a joke," said Dinah, looking almost genuinely sorry.

"What do you mean, JOKE?" I cried, foaming at the mouth. My witchy blood was up, I can tell you.

"Well, " said Dinah, keeping her distance. "I just thought it would be fun at first and then the thing with the trumpet happened and I thought... well, I thought fate had taken a hand and given us a chance to put things right for you. "And if you remember, I tried to cancel it all one time, by NOT talking. And you got really UPSET. And so I gave in and pretended Lorenzo told Harpo not to do the show."

"Oh. Yeah. I remember," I said. "That was the time I hit you with a pillow full of Duplo."

"Exactly. I was fighting for my life... And if I HAD admitted it, you would have cancelled the show, and..." she trailed to an un-Dinah like stop.

At that very moment, the door bell rang.

It was Mrs Next-Door, Very Extremely excited. As you have probably already noticed, she is one of those owners who treat their dogs like children and Lorenzo's puppies, even though they only have humble old Harpo for a mum, have made her feel like a proud granny.

"I must speak to your mother immediately, Trixie," she said. Oh no. What have I done now?

"Oh Trix, what have you done now?" said Mum, rushing out and trying to straighten the mat, which was hard, as Mrs Next-Door, who is not a small lady, was standing on it. Mrs Next-Door always makes you feel like straightening mats and stuff because her house is like nothing has ever moved in it for centuries.

But it was good news.

"Look!" said Mrs Next-Door. "I've found your Diamond Togetherness Ring! It was at the bottom of Lorenzo's basket!"

Me and Dinah and Chloe all looked at each other with smiles too big for our faces. Surely Harpo must have given Lorenzo the ring!

Maybe Harpo can't talk, but she sure knows how to fall in love.

Mum and Mrs Next-Door went joyfully into the kitchen to have a heart-warming cuppa and crow over the puppies. They were like two old grannies together.

Maybe the clouds are lifting, I thought to myself. But there's still the trumpet...

The doorbell rang again. Mum and Mrs Next-Door were wittering over the puppies and didn't hear it. I looked through the window to see who it was.

Horrors! Horrors! It was the strange old bearded man from the bus, who'd been following me. He'd found out where I live!

"What is it?" said Chloe and Dinah together, seeing the look on my face.

"It's him!" I groaned, clutching them. "He's a wizard in a dirty hat, a devil in a donkey jacket! Everywhere I go he follows me!"

The door bell rang again. This time Mum and Mrs Next-Door heard it.

"Trixie," called my mum. "See who's at the door, will you?"

I crouched in the front room, frozen to the spot, the others frozen to me. He knew someone was in now, he must have heard Mum's voice.

The door bell rang yet again. Aaaaaargghh! What were we going to DO?

"Patricia!" shouted Mum again. "For goodness sake answer the door!"

I didn't move. I couldn't move. There was a long silence. And then...

"FAAAARNNNNNNNNN!" An extraordinary noise, like an elephant with a sore throat, bellowing, filled the room.

Mum and Mrs Next-Door stopped talking.

"What on earth was that?" I heard Mum say.

"WNNNNAAHHHHHMMMMM!" went the extraordinary elephant noise again.

A strange cackle, like a rusty machine starting up that hasn't been used for years, started coming from behind the front door. Mum came out into the hall and went towards the door, a bit dubiously.

"Don't open it!" I shouted, finding my voice.

Then I saw Dad through the window, turning in at the gate.

"Dad's here!" I screamed at Mum, clutching my beloved Bonzo to my chest. Mum wrenched open the door to see what was going on, just as another elephant sound:

"Babaaaannnnnnnhhhhh," was dying away. And then we all saw what was making it.

Looking even more sinister and fearsome, the old man was lowering my trumpet from his mouth. "Want this back do you?" he asked, his voice like a dry hinge.

Dad and Mum looked at me, completely baffled.

"What does he mean?" asked Dad, looking warily at the old man.

"She knows," he said, meaningfully. "But it ought to be fair exchange, oughtn't it? That's a nice puppy you've got there come to think of it, be a nice companion for me in my old age."

My witchy blood surged. **"NEVER,"** I cried. "You can have my **LIFE SAVINGS!"** And I raced upstairs to raid my Merlin fund. Four whole years of saving... I took out £40, which left just £7.84p. I ran downstairs and furiously thrust it at the old man. "Here, take my life savings," I snarled.

I began to realise, distraught as I was, that somehow the atmosphere had changed since I ran upstairs. There were smiles on Mum's and Dad's faces. Dinah and Chloe were sniggering. I didn't understand.

But he took the money.

My heart sank. Merlin galloped away into the wide blue yonder.

The rusty laughter returned. He held out the trumpet to me. "Used to play one of these when I was a lad," he said, smiling what suddenly started to look like quite a nice smile at me. "Can't do it so well these days, without the puff or the teeth."

I was struck dumb. But Dinah didn't look

surprised any more. Nor did Chloe. Nor did Mum and Dad, and Mrs Next-Door, who had obviously been told something I didn't know.

"I've been trying to give you this back for the past two days," said the old man. "You left it on the bus. And here's your change."

I stretched out my hand, shaking, for my trumpet.

He gave me back £39.50p too. Said he needed 50p for the bus fare.

Merlin tossed his golden head and galloped back.

"Thank you very much," I said, very meekly indeed.

"Cheers," said the Very Extremely Nice Old Man who, I suddenly noticed, didn't smell of anything but pipe-tobacco – and apart from a missing tooth or three and clothes that he'd obviously had to keep in service for a very long time, looked as nice as, well, Father Christmas. Nicer, really.

"Cheers," I said, hugging Bonzo.

"Phew, thanks," whispered Bonzo, when we were alone. "I'm too young to leave home."